W9-BNU-767

WITHDRAWN

101

LOUDMOUTH GEORGE and the SIXTH-GRADE BULLY

LoudMOUTH GEORGE and the SIXTH-GRADE BULLY

NANCY ★ CARLSON

Carolrhoda Books, Inc. / Minneapolis

For Lloyd, who has survived the bullies of the world

Text and illustrations copyright © 1983 by Nancy Carlson, © 2003 by Nancy Carlson

All rights reserved. International copyright secured. No part of this book may be reproduced, stored in a retrieval system, or transmitted in any form or by any means—electronic, mechanical, photocopying, recording, or otherwise—without the prior written permission of Carolrhoda Books, Inc., except for the inclusion of brief quotations in an acknowledged review.

This book is available in two editions:
Library binding by Carolrhoda Books, Inc., a division of Lerner Publishing Group
Soft cover by First Avenue Editions, an imprint of Lerner Publishing Group
241 First Avenue North
Minneapolis, MN 55401 U.S.A.

Website address: www.lernerbooks.com

Library of Congress Cataloging-in-Publication Data

Carlson, Nancy L.
    Loudmouth George and the sixth-grade bully / written and illustrated
by Nancy Carlson.—20th Anniversary ed.
        p.   cm.
    Summary: After having his lunch repeatedly stolen by a bully twice his size,
Loudmouth George and his friend Harriet teach the bully a lesson he'll
never forget.
    ISBN: 1–57505–218–0 (lib. bdg. : alk. paper)
    ISBN: 1–57505–549–X (pbk. : alk. paper)
    1. [Bullies—Fiction. 2. Rabbits—Fiction]. I. Title.
PZ7.C21665 Lq 2003
    [E]—dc21   2002009205

Manufactured in the United States of America
1 2 3 4 5 6 – JR – 08 07 06 05 04 03

It was the first day of school. George was excited.

Suddenly an enormous sixth grader jumped out of the bushes. George had never seen him before, but he knew right away that this must be Big Mike, the new kid in town.

"Hi-ya, squirt," said Big Mike. "Gimme all your money or I won't let you by."

"I don't have any money," said George.

"Then gimme your lunch."

"You call this a lunch?" yelled Big Mike. "You'd better have something better than this tomorrow! Now get out of here."

George ran faster than he ever had before.

That day George had nothing to eat for lunch.
"Forget your lunch?" said Harriet. "Here, you
can have half of my peanut butter sandwich."

After school George raced home. He was afraid
Big Mike would be waiting for him.

That night he ate an enormous dinner.

"Goodness, you're hungry this evening," said George's mother.

"Maybe you'd better pack me a bigger lunch tomorrow?" said George.

The next morning Big Mike took George's lunch again.

"Listen, Big Ears," he said, "you'd better have more cookies tomorrow."

That day George had nothing to eat for lunch again.

"Golly, George, I already ate my sandwich," said Harriet. "You're sure getting forgetful."

The next morning George sneaked some extra cookies into his lunch box. Then he took the long way to school, but Big Mike caught him anyway.

"Don't get tricky with me, Twitch Nose," said Big Mike as he grabbed George's lunch.

By the end of the week George was a nervous
wreck. He couldn't pay attention in class, he
jumped when anyone called his name, and he was
hungry all the time.

"Something fishy is going on here," said Harriet on Friday. "You'd better tell me what it is, George."

So George told Harriet the whole story. He felt
a little better then, but not much.

"We should tell the principal," said Harriet.
"It won't do any good," said George. "Big Mike
doesn't go to this school."

"Hmmm," said Harriet. "I think I have an idea.
Meet me at my house tomorrow morning."

Saturday morning George biked over to Harriet's.
He shook all the way there.

"Here's the plan," said Harriet, and she whispered
into George's ear as she pulled him into the kitchen.

The two of them set to work making a lunch.
First they made two tunafish sandwiches. They
poured half a jar of garlic powder into the tunafish.

Then they filled a thermos halfway with vegetable soup. They filled it the rest of the way with vinegar.

Then they mixed hot pepper into some fruit cocktail and put it in a jar.

Finally they separated some cream-filled cookies. They ate the frosting, then filled the cookies with lard instead.

Then they went to see Harriet's cousin, Lance.

On Monday morning George hid his real lunch in his school bag and carried the lunch he and Harriet had made. Then he set off for school. Lance followed close behind but kept out of sight.

Sure enough, Big Mike stole George's lunch again.

"Won't he be surprised," said George. "I sure taught that Big Mike a lesson!"

But just to be on the safe side, George had Lance
follow him to school for the rest of the week.